OVER
THE RIVER
AND THROUGH
THE WOOD

illustrated by Emma Randall

Penguin Workshop

An Imprint of Penguin Random House

Over the river, and through the wood,
to Grandmother's house we go.

The horse knows the way to carry the sleigh

through the white and drifted snow.

Over the river,
and through the wood,
to Grandmother's
house away!

We would not stop for doll or top,

for 'tis Thanksgiving Day.

Over the river, and through the wood—

oh, how the wind does blow!

It stings the toes and bites the nose
as over the ground we go.

Over the river, and through the wood—

and straight through
the barnyard gate.

We seem to go
extremely slow;
it is so hard to wait!

Over the river, and
through the wood—

when Grandmother sees us come,
she will say,

"Oh dear, the children are here.
Bring a pie for everyone."

Over the river,
and through the wood—
now Grandmother's cap I spy!

Hurrah for the fun! Is the pudding done?
Hurrah for the pumpkin pie!

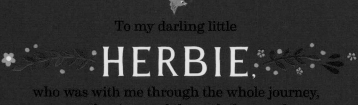

To my darling little

HERBIE,

who was with me through the whole journey,
over the river and through the woods
of this book.

PENGUIN WORKSHOP

Penguin Young Readers Group
An Imprint of Penguin Random House LLC

Illustrations copyright © 2018 by Emma Randall. All rights reserved. Published by Penguin Workshop,
an imprint of Penguin Random House LLC, 345 Hudson Street, New York, New York 10014.
PENGUIN and PENGUIN WORKSHOP are trademarks of Penguin Books Ltd, and the
W colophon is a trademark of Penguin Random House LLC. Manufactured in China.

Library of Congress Cataloging-in-Publication Data is available.

ISBN 9780515157659   10 9 8 7 6 5 4 3 2 1